SLOW DOWN SAMMY

First Published 2024 by Snowdrop Publishing
www.Snowdrop-Publishing.com

ISBN: 978-1-916703-08-7
Copyright © Natasha Iregbu

The right of Natasha Iregbu and Natacha Galbano to be identified as the author and illustrator of this work has been asserted by them in accordance with the Copyright, Designs and Patents Act 1988.

All rights reserved. No part of this publication may be reproduced, stored in a retrieval system, or transmitted, in any form, or by any means, without the prior written permission of the author.

Thank you to...

Eleanor Baggaley and Natacha Galbano for their work in bringing Slow Down Sammy to life.

Louise Shanagher for her teachings from The Creative Mindfulness Method.

Last but not least, to you for choosing to read Slow Down Sammy.

This book belongs to

_____
_____
_____
_____

Amaya was excited to play with her best friend Sammy.

When she saw him, she noticed his petals were closed.

"Sammy, are you sleeping?" Amaya whispered.

He didn't answer.

"Sammy?" She wondered if he was ok.

"Hello Amaya," he replied, "I'm awake."

Sammy slowly opened his petals.

"I'm happy to see you again," Amaya smiled, "how are you today?"

"I...I'm worried and feel a little anxious," Sammy whispered.

"Wow! That's exciting!" Amaya exclaimed.

Sammy didn't feel excited.

"What if no one votes for me? I...I don't want to lose," he stuttered while turning away. "I feel like I have butterflies in my tummy."

Amaya told Sammy, "It's ok to feel worried. I sometimes get worried too."

"Really?" he turned back round.

"Yup, I worry about talking too much," she shrugged.

Sammy kept listening.

"I'll vote for you. You might even win, you never know what could happen!" Amaya gushed.

He looked confused, "I didn't think about winning."

"We don't know what will happen in the future. We only know what is happening in each moment," Amaya explained.

"Do you know what that means?"

Sammy shook his head.

She continued, "When you are in the moment, you can notice when your worries come into your mind. Then let them float away again."

"But letting go of worries is hard," Sammy sighed.

"It is," Amaya agreed, "but worries don't last forever; they come and go like all the other emotions."

Sammy liked the idea that worries don't last forever.

"You talked to me about your worries, which is one way to let go of them," she reassured Sammy.

Sammy felt less worried already. "Thank you for listening to me," he told Amaya.

Amaya had an idea.

"Do you want to play the 5, 4, 3, 2, 1 game with me?" she asked.

"Yes, let's play."

"Yay! Let's take 3 deep breaths."

She slowly counted, "One… Two…Three…"

"Ready to start?"

Sammy nodded.

"Ok. What are five things you can see?"

Sammy looked around. "I can see you, the grass, a ladybird, clouds and the sun."

"Well done. It's your turn to ask me!" Amaya exclaimed.

"What four things can you touch?"

"Hmmm," she paused, "my wings, the wind, this leaf, and my feet."

"I'll ask you now. What three things can you hear?" Amaya asked.

He listened carefully, "The wind, birds and a bumblebee."

"I can hear them too!" she exclaimed.

Sammy asked Amaya, "What are two things you can smell?"

She breathed in deeply, "Lavender from those plants, and I can smell your petals."

"Last question, Sammy...What is one thing you can taste?"

"That's easy," he smiled. "Nectar. It tastes yummy."

"Yum! That was so much fun," said Amaya, "Maybe we could play it at the flower contest."

"That would be fun," Sammy replied.

Amaya fluttered her wings "I play the 5, 4, 3, 2, 1 game by myself when I get worried."

"Do you?!" Sammy was surprised.

"Yup, it always helps me feel nice and relaxed."

Sammy smiled. He felt relieved that he had shared his worry with Amaya.

"I can see the sunset," Amaya announced, "My mummy told me to come home when the sunset comes. I'll see you soon Sammy."

"Bye-bye," Sammy waved, "Thanks for coming to play."

Do you ever feel worried?

It's ok to feel worried. It's not a right or wrong way to feel. We all have emotions and feeling worried is one of them.

When you practice mindfulness, it helps bring your attention to what is happening in the moment.

Whenever your mind is busy with worries, you can try the '5, 4, 3, 2, 1 Method'. That's the game Sammy and Amaya played in the story.

Would you like to try it with Sammy?

Close your eyes or look towards the ground.

If you can't use all your senses, use the senses you have.

Take a deep breath in through your nose and count to three.

One... Two... Three...

Now, slowly breathe out through your mouth.

Open your eyes or look up from the ground.

What 5 things can you see?

What 4 things can you touch?

What 3 things can you hear?

What 2 things can you smell?

What is 1 thing you can taste?

How do you feel?

Who can you talk to about your feelings?
Write or draw 5 people.

How do you feel after sharing your worries with someone?
Draw a picture.

What is your favourite way to relax?

What would you say to someone who is feeling worried?

About the Author

Natasha Iregbu is an Author, Mindfulness Teacher and Coach, Yoga Teacher and Community Education Worker.

Natasha helps support children's wellbeing by sharing mindfulness in a fun and accessible way. Her first book, Slow Down Amaya, is shortlisted in the Ink Book Prize 2024.

Find out more about Natasha and her books at www.butterfly-minds.co.uk

www.ingramcontent.com/pod-product-compliance
Lightning Source LLC
Chambersburg PA
CBHW041540040426
42446CB00002B/165